TOAD

For Christopher F.

ISBN 0-439-13356-4

Copyright © 1996 by Ruth Brown. All rights reserved.
Published by Scholastic Inc., 555 Broadway, New York, NY 10012,
by arrangement with Dutton Children's Books, a division of Penguin Putnam Inc.
SCHOLASTIC and associated logos are trademarks and/or registered
trademarks of Scholastic Inc.

12 11 10 9 8 7 6 5 4 3 2 1   9/9 0 1 2 3 4/0

Printed in the U.S.A.   24

First Scholastic printing, March 1999

Originally published in Great Britain 1996 by Andersen Press Ltd., London.

Typography by Lillian Rosenstreich

TOAD

Ruth Brown

SCHOLASTIC INC.

New York Toronto London Auckland Sydney
Mexico City New Delhi Hong Kong

This is the tale of a toad.

A muddy toad, a mucky toad,
a clammy, sticky, gooey toad,

odorous, oozing, foul and filthy,
and dripping with venomous fluid.

Toad's covered in warts and lumps
and bumps, with stains and
spots and speckled humps.

He's nasty, septic, toxic, and bitter,
and he leaves a slimy trail.

Toad is also a bug-crunching toad—
a greedy, fly-munching, worm-slurping toad.

He is clumsy and careless, sluggish and slow,

and he can't even see very well.
So, winking and blinking,
he waddles and stumbles,
trudges and trundles

straight into the jaws of a monster!

Yuuuuuck!

yells the monster.
It spits out the toad—

the happy toad, the safe toad,
the carefree and self-confident toad,

the toad with a monstrous smile.